This book belongs to

. . . .

The Baby Dragon

~Tamer

Jan Fearnley

EGMONT

One dark and starry night,
when a baby was sleeping in his bed . . .

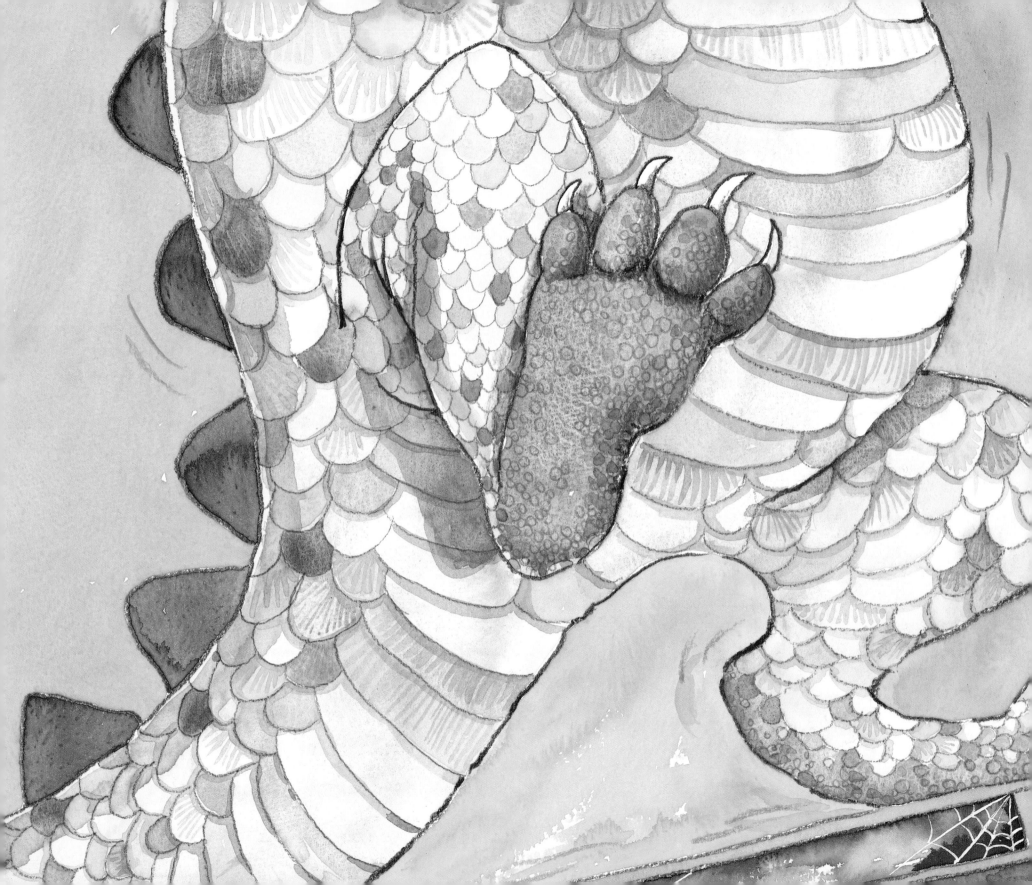

. . . along came a *great big dragon*,
looking for treasure.

STAMP!
STAMP!
CRASH!

Went his feet.

Went the furniture.

Books flew like birds.

Walls trembled like jelly.

The dragon snorted
silver sparks.
He farted purple smoke.
He was full of magic and fire
and bad, bad temper.

This rumpus woke
the baby up.

He rubbed his eyes,
blinked
and went to see
what the fuss
was about.

Through
silver wisps
of smoke,

the dragon glared
at the baby.
"Give me your
treasure!" he demanded.

"Bleah!" said the baby.

"Hey, I'm mean and nasty,"
growled the dragon.
"You should be very frightened.
GIVE ME YOUR TREASURE!"

"Goo-goo!" said the baby.
(He didn't know how
to be frightened.
He was too little.)

The dragon frowned.

"Why," he said,
"this cheeky little flea
thinks he can take me on!
All-righty, I'll show you."

The dragon threw
back his head and
roared a terrifying roar:

RRRAAAAAAAAA

GH!

"I bet you can't do that," he smirked, patting the baby on the back.

rraagh!

burped the baby.

"Harrumph. Very impressive," said the dragon. "But watch this."

He screwed up his face and puffed out
fire and sparks, which sizzled in the air.

"NOW, GIVE ME

YOUR TREASURE!" he cried.

"Tee-hee," went the baby, flapping his arms with delight.

Then he screwed up his face like a little old apple.

Prrroooooooop!

"Whatever next!" said the dragon.

He soon found out.

"This isn't treasure," he said,
wrestling with a nappy,
powder and pins.
"This certainly
isn't treasure."

Then the dragon showed the baby his biggest,
best and scariest trick of all.

With a flap of his scaly wings,
together they hurtled through the dark, dark sky.

They waved to the big yellow moon
and said hello to the twinkly stars.

"Wheeeeee!" said the baby.

Safely back home, the baby was sad.
He LOVED flying!

"Waah!" he cried.

"Oh, no!" said the dragon.
He had never heard such
a terrible noise.

"Don't cry, baby.
Just give me
your treasure."

But the baby kept crying: "Waaaah!"

So the dragon
played him a tune . . .

. . . danced him a dance . . .

. . . and did some tricks . . .

But every time he stopped,
the baby cried.

The poor dragon didn't know what to do.

Then he had an idea.

Ever so gently,
he picked up the baby
and cradled him
like a precious jewel.

The baby smiled trustingly
into the dragon's
emerald eyes.

The dragon smiled back.

It was pure magic.

And as the baby chuckled and snuggled in the dragon's big strong arms, the huge beast's heart was filled with love.

"There, there my little treasure," whispered the dragon.

The dragon decided
he would like to stay.

"You've given me something
so precious," he said.
"Would you like me to teach you
something special?"

"All-righty!"
said the baby.